Balboa Press books may be ordered through booksellers or by contacting:

Balboa Press
A Division of Hay House
1663 Liberty Drive
Bloomington, IN 47403
www.balboapress.com.au
1 (877) 407-4847

ISBN: 978-1-5043-1549-4 (sc)
978-1-5043-1548-7 (e)

Print information available on the last page.

Balboa Press rev. date: 10/30/2018

BALBOA
PRESS
A DIVISION OF HAY HOUSE

Ellie

the Hen Afraid of
Worms

KIRA BRETTSCHNEIDER

Ellie was a big brown hen and
it was plain to see

She was afraid of worms,

Oh dear me!

You see, when Ellie saw a worm it didn't have the normal features,

Her head turned it into ferocious looking creatures.

Her best friend Dani

Would get her to walk around and around.

But at the sight of a worm she would freeze

And drop to the ground.

Together, Ellie and Dani would
roam far and wide

In search of a cure.

But what they found was nothing
more than manure.

Dani said to Ellie, "I know what we can do?

Let's go and search the wide open
spaces for a fear fix clue."

The hens took off out into the world to see who could help.

Their first stop was a turkey, but all he did was make them yelp.

"Oh Dani, what can I do it seems so crazy,

To be afraid of something that
spends its days all hazy."

"You're not too worry my friend," Dani did say.

"Let's try again tomorrow, after
all it is another day."

Again the hens did wander, to
the next poultry quack.

A lovely golden pheasant, but
she just sent them back.

Their spirits were getting low,
it buried them way down.

To walk amongst the others who'd
just snicker and frown.

The following day Dani came flapping,

"Ellie, Ellie, I've got it. I know what we can do.

It's out the back, along the track
near the old wooden pew.

The two set off with confidence
and a little smile,

Ready to discover what would
take away the bile.

And near the pew a drake
named Henry did say,

"Welcome dear ladies let's be rid of
the fear and go about our day."

"Ellie, I need you to close your eyes and rock.

Use your minds' eye to find a worm and cluck."

"Cluck like you've never clucked before."

"It's working" she did say, "more, more, more."

"Now float down and look upon
the tiny brown worm

And say, 'You're nothing but a
tasty delicious germ!'"

Open your eyes and what do you see?

Henry was holding a wriggly
worm, Oh dear me.

But Ellie licked her lips the look
of fear and panic and glum

Was all gone instead all she said was "Yum!"

Ellie turned to Henry with a cheeky, tiny smile

"You've fixed me I know what to do.

Peck and scratch and flap around
for my fear is now adieu."

The sun was sinking low as the
ladies left the duck.

Aware now at just how much food
was waiting in the muck.

Printed in the United States
By Bookmasters